BOMBAY
Ever After

LOVE
HUDSON-MAGGIO

Published by Sweet Auburn Publishing

This book is a work of fiction. The characters, incidents, and dialogue are drawn from the author's imagination and are not to be construed as real. Any resemblance to actual events or persons, living or dead, is entirely coincidental.

Any internet addresses (websites, blogs, etc.) in this book are offered as a resource. They are not intended in any way to be or imply an endoursement by Sweet Auburn Publishing, nor does Sweet Auburn Publishing vouch for the content of these sites for the life of this book.

Library of Congress Cataloging-in-Publication Data is on file.
ISBN: 979-8-9920953-4-0 (paperback)
ISBN: 979-8-9920953-5-7 (eBook)

Printed in the United States of America

To my readers—
You are the reason these stories exist. Your messages, your photos with my books, and the quiet joy you share after finishing a chapter keep me writing. Bombay Ever After is my gift to you—for every late-night reader who believed in second chances and the magic of imperfect love.

To my family and friends—
Thank you for your unshakable faith in me. For listening to drafts at odd hours, cheering me on through deadlines, and reminding me that storytelling is not just what I do—it's who I am. You've been my grounding when I doubted, my laughter when I needed light, and my constant proof that love—in all its forms—is worth writing about.

With gratitude and all my heart,
Love

THE OTHER FLAME

A Desi retelling of *The Great Gatsby* with glamour, soul,
and a new ending because I love a happy ending…

ACT I—MONSOON ARRIVAL

CHAPTER ONE

The House Next to Shah's

In June of 2025, just before the monsoon drenched Bombay like silk spilled from the sky, I moved into a villa behind the Colaba Causeway. It had once belonged to a Portuguese merchant's widow—now it belonged to me, Kabir Deshmukh, a startup dropout with too much time and just enough regret.

I had sold my app, escaped my engagement, and washed up here with the other flotsam. Everyone said I should rest. Instead, I watched the neighbors.

My villa was modest: ivy-covered colonial bones, chipped tiles, shuttered windows that rattled in the wind. But next door?

Next door was a legend.

Jay Shah lived there. The Jay Shah. Hotel magnate, investment sorcerer, the man whose name moved real estate prices like weather.

Elaborate NY opera house sets paled in comparison to his house. Mango trees framed the white facade, while brass lanterns glowed behind high windows. Every Saturday night, the music began. The evening soundtrack filtered through the palms, a vague movie score of conversation, clinking glasses, the occasional gasp, and annoying raucous laughter from that one guest who's always too loud and too drunk.

People said his parties were curated—not wild, not boisterous—curated, as if each guest had been chosen for maximum contrast.

But no one ever saw Jay Shah. At least not until I did.

CHAPTER TWO

First Glimpses

She arrived in week three. She didn't knock. She didn't announce herself. She slipped in the side—the secret you'd put aside just far enough to begin to forget.

She stepped out of a matte-black Mercedes wearing a cream-colored sari edged in rose gold. Her earrings danced when she turned her head. Her smile, the one she shared with the doorman and bystanders, was the sort people practice alone in mirrors.

Someone whispered her name. It floated across my face with the scent of vanilla extract and the slight brush of a thorn: Diya Kapoor.

Daughter of a diplomat. Married to a Delhi financier with ancestral titles and newer sins. Seen on red carpets in Milan, fundraisers in Singapore, temples in Varanasi, she carried herself with a panther's grace and the gravitas of ancestral privilege.

Another voice nearby whispered, "Jay Shah loved her once."

The evening's music sounded softer—*ghazal* poetry set to rhythm and oozing from the honeyed throat of an unseen soloist. The warm, damp air was further weighted by the lyrics: *raat bhar tera intezaar kiya…*"I waited for you all night."

From my perch on the balcony, I watched elongated shadows shift and wondered if Diya Kapoor danced. I wondered if she even needed to.

CHAPTER THREE

The Man Behind the Myth

It wasn't at a party that I met Jay. It was during a blackout.

The storm arrived without ceremony, splitting power lines and flinging coconuts from trees. My house dimmed to silence. I had just typed and deleted the same sentence for the twelfth time when there was a knock.

I opened the door to find a barefoot man in a rain-soaked kurta, hair slicked back, eyes bright.

"Jay Shah," he said, as though he weren't.

He smiled. "Your lights are out. We have a backup generator next door. And Lagavulin 16."

That's how I met him—myth undone, glass in hand, seated beside a fireplace that didn't need to be lit. His living room had teak paneling, velvet cushions, and a playlist of old Hindustani jazz perfuming the air.

He didn't talk business. He talked about silence. About monsoons. About how he hated art that screamed and preferred it to whisper.

I liked him immediately.

It would be weeks before I understood that every word he spoke had been chosen like those on an engraved invitation.

CHAPTER FOUR

The Woman He Built For

She was everywhere in Jay's house. Not in photos—he was far too careful for that. But in scent. In sound. In the way he looked toward the piano when music played.

"She was my beginning," he said once, pouring another finger of single malt during another blackout. "And now she's the echo I keep rebuilding for."

He never used her name. But I didn't need it.

Diya came often. Always unexpected. Once in rainboots, once in Chanel. Always in white, like she feared color might give her away.

They never touched. But their silences rumbled with the warning of distant thunder.

Her husband was rarely present. He existed more as a footnote—a powerful man's idea of possession.

But Jay said nothing against him. That was his style. Never accuse. Only wait.

When Diya left the house one evening, she looked back—not at me, though I was watching. At Jay.

And in her glance, I recognized something fragile. Something that said, *Please remember me softer than when I left.*

ACT II—THE INVITATION

CHAPTER FIVE

Something Like Destiny

I met Diya at Kala Ghoda Café on a Sunday that smelled like cinnamon and wet leaves. She wore no makeup, no jewelry—just a cotton kurta and the kind of confidence that doesn't need pronouncements.

"You're Kabir," she said, sliding into the chair across from mine. "The one who reads Tagore and pretends not to listen."

"And you're the storm everyone else tries to predict," I replied, half-smiling.

She tilted her head. "Do you believe in second chances?"

It was too early for questions like that. But Diya asked everything like she already knew the answer.

"I think second chances are just better-timed first ones."

She smiled like I'd said something she wasn't ready to believe.

"I'm hosting a dinner," she said. "Eight guests. Rooftop of Sea Palace. Jay will be there. I want you to come."

It was not a request. So, for the first time since I arrived in Bombay, I said yes without hesitation.

CHAPTER SIX

The Dinner at the Edge of the Sea

The scent of orange blossoms drifted along the paper lanterns that hung over a mosaic-tiled patio. A monsoon breeze, salty and secretive, curled around our ankles.

Jay was already there, backlit by city lights, dressed in ink-blue with an open collar and an unsure smile.

Diya made her entrance at the precise, just-before-she-was-too-late moment.

She wore a black sari that swallowed the night. She had a silver cuff around one wrist and no husband clutching the other. She made no excuses but glided in with an authority and an unspoken announcement in my distant memory: "She walks in beauty like the night…" entrance that invited poetry.

Dinner was all politeness, curated laughter, and dishes passed with casual grace.

But beneath the performance, something flickered.

Jay poured her wine. She didn't meet his eyes.

She told a story about getting lost in Istanbul. He corrected the city. She laughed and told him not to be boring.

After dessert, most of the guests retreated to the edge for photos and flirtation.

Only the three of us remained.

"I remember everything," Diya said suddenly, voice low.

Jay's fingers tightened around his glass. "Even the things you said you forgot?"

She nodded. "Especially those."

She stood, brushing invisible wrinkles from her sari. "Goodnight."

Neither of us moved until she was gone.

CHAPTER SEVEN

The Storm in August

Scandal arrived the way it always does in Bombay: fast, glossy, and far too late.

Photos leaked.

Jay and Diya on his balcony. Her hand on his chest. His lips inches from her hair.

They weren't kissing. But they weren't pretending.

Tabloids howled. News anchors speculated. Her husband fled to Singapore.

Jay didn't respond.

Shah House went dark for eight days.

On the ninth, Diya came to my door.

She looked nothing like the woman in the papers.

She looked real.

"I don't want to be a headline," she said.

We walked the sea wall in silence.

"I thought marriage would make me safe," she said. "I thought tradition would soften into comfort. But it just hardened into expectation."

"And Jay?" I asked.

She didn't answer right away.

Finally, she whispered, "Jay is the life I wanted. I just didn't know I was allowed to want it."

We stood in the drizzle, not speaking.

Sometimes truth needs no punctuation.

ACT III—THE CHOICE

CHAPTER EIGHT
The Last Party

It was the final Saturday of August, and the sky held its breath.

Jay Shah's invitations went out in gold-foiled boxes containing hand-painted escort cards, perfumed with vetiver and bergamot. No publicists. No influencers. Only those who had weathered the season, socially and emotionally.

It was his last party, and everyone felt it.

The mansion gleamed like a monument to something ending. Chandeliers dripped crystals. Musicians played on a marble dais festooned with lotus motifs. Guests arrived in silks and sequins, draped in heritage diamonds, ankle bells, and tension.

And then Diya entered.

She wore red.

Not the dusty rose of nostalgia. Not the coral of safe elegance. But scarlet—alive, defiant, brilliant as a promise. The blouse was sleeveless, her back bare, her hair pinned high in a crown of floral elegance. She had no silver cuff.

She sported no wedding band.

All of Colaba paused.

Jay saw her across the lawn, and for the first time in a decade, he moved. No waiting. No performance. He walked straight to her, bypassing ministers and models, past patrons and ghosts.

They met at the center of the garden beneath a tree wrapped in lights.

No words. Just breathe. Just eyes.

Just the truth, shared in silence.

CHAPTER NINE

The Decision

I watched them from the shadows, the ice in my glass ruining my scotch.

Diya placed her hand on Jay's shoulder. Her fingers curved like a memory returning home, but gripping as if she wasn't entirely sure the ground would hold.

They danced. Not a waltz or any other recognizable step. Nothing choreographed. Just… movement. Two people chose gravity in a room that only rewarded illusion.

Afterward, she found me near the pool.

"Everyone thinks I came back for him," she said.

"You didn't?"

She took a breath. "I came back for myself. Loving Jay was never the hard part. Believing I was allowed to choose has taken me ten years."

The rain began to pester us. The monsoon's untidy farewell.

"I'm not going back," she said.

"To your husband?"

"To whom I was supposed to be."

She smiled—not for Jay, or for the crowd, or even for me. It was for her.

CHAPTER TEN

Jay

Jay stood on the edge of his veranda the next morning, hair tousled, kurta still rumpled from the night before.

"She stayed," he said.

I nodded. "She chose you."

"No," he said. "She chose herself. I was just lucky to be where she landed."

He handed me a cup of chai. No Lagavulin today.

"I spent ten years building this house for a woman I thought I'd lost. But what I really built was the courage to deserve her when she returned."

"She always knew," I said.

He smiled. "But I needed to know too."

CHAPTER ELEVEN

Kabir

I stayed in the villa next door. The city settled. Monsoon season slipped off stage like an exhausted performer.

I wrote again. Not code. Not investor decks. Just words. Memory. Truth.

Sometimes I'd see Jay and Diya walking barefoot in the garden, trading poems in languages they no longer needed translated. Other times, I saw only the light from their window and knew they were there, choosing each other.

I was no longer lost. I was no longer watching.

I was writing the ending.

EPILOGUE

Love in the Present Tense

They moved to a smaller house in Alibaug. No security gates. No staff. Just space.

Diya opened an art school for girls. Jay started a boutique hotel that didn't need a name.

And I finally learned the difference between witnessing a love story and living one.

And in Bombay, where everything ends in a monsoon, I discovered the rarest thing:

A beginning.

THE MARRYING KIND

Welcome to the world where love defies borders, tradition meets rebellion, and no heart leaves unchanged.

At a luxurious wellness retreat in the Western Ghats, Anya Kapoor, longtime family friend of Vikram Chatwal, faces the man she once left behind: Sameer Malhotra, now a self-made tech mogul. When he checks in as a guest, years of buried love, regret, and longing surface under the peaceful exterior.

"You can bury the past in eucalyptus and silence.
But when it knocks again, what will you say?"

ACT I—WHAT WE LEFT BEHIND

CHAPTER ONE

Shantivan Wellness Retreat sat high in the misty folds of the Western Ghats, a haven of emerald jungles and pinpointed luxury. At dawn, the hills wore a silvery veil of mist. It clung to the rainforest canopy and the tiled roofs of the retreat's villas with the fervor or a free climber clutching a belay. The air was cool and heady with the scent of damp earth and frangipani blossoms.

Anya Kapoor moved along the flagstone path that wound between yoga pavilions and lotus ponds, mentally ticking off final details. To the casual observer, she was serene and in control, the picture of an elegant resort founder ensuring perfection for her high-profile guests.

In the soft morning light, Anya's tailored linen kurta and immaculate creamy ivory trousers set off her warm brown skin. Her long ebony hair gathered at her neck in a low bun, not a strand out of place. At thirty years old, she exuded a composed grace that made every member of the bustling staff slow in deference when she passed.

A young attendant greeted as he adjusted a bamboo lantern along the path. "Good morning, ma'am." Anya offered a polite smile and a quiet "Namaste" in return, her tone gentle but authoritative. "Please remember to have the welcome drinks chilled by noon."

Despite her calm exterior, Anya's stomach fluttered with a strange unease this morning. The retreat's grand opening for a week-long wellness event was hours away, and everything was on track—yet she felt an inexplicable tension coiling beneath her practiced composure. She paused at the reception gazebo overlooking a valley blanketed in rainforest. She inhaled deeply, anticipating the calls of distant birds and the babble of a hillside stream would ground her nerves. Normally, this panorama of lush green slopes and distant waterfalls steadied her. Why, then, did she feel as if something was about to upend her carefully ordered world?

A familiar voice called out and pulled her from her thoughts. "Anya!"

Jaya Singh—her cousin and closest confidante—approached with two steaming cups of ginger chai. Jaya was a few years younger, with a bright smile and an easy warmth that put everyone at ease. Today her affability was tempered with concern. She handed Anya a cup. "You're up early double-checking everything, hmm? The itinerary is set, the staff is prepped. You've got this." Jaya nudged her cousin's arm playfully. "Even the weather is behaving—no surprise monsoons for our VIP guests."

Anya mustered a small smile and took a grateful sip. The spiced tea soothed her, and she tried to focus on Jaya's encouraging words. "I know. It's not my first retreat, but... this one is different." She frowned slightly, gazing down into her cup. They had hosted celebrities and business magnates before, but this week's guest list was particularly elite. "We have the Minister of Tourism coming, and that Bollywood starlet, what's her name... and a bunch of global CEOs flying in." Anya enumerated the guests as if the sheer importance of each added weight to her anxiety.

Jaya's eyes sparkled mischievously over the rim of her cup. "Speaking of the guest list," she said lightly, "there was one name I wanted to ask you about." She set her chai down and flipped open the leather-bound register sitting on the reception desk. With a perfectly manicured finger, Jaya traced down the list of names. "Here. Sameer Malhotra. He RSVP'd late, just yesterday. I nearly missed it." She glanced up carefully to catch Anya's reaction. "Any idea if it's *that* Sameer Malhotra?"

At the sound of the name, Anya's heart gave a traitorous thump against her ribcage. Her fingers tightened imperceptibly around her teacup. She hoped her face remained impassive.

"Sameer Malhotra is a common name," she said evenly, but her voice was a touch too soft. Inside, her mind was already racing. She stepped closer to Jaya and peered at the elegant script on the page. *Sameer Malhotra—Silicon Valley.* The note beside the name confirmed it: *This is indeed him.* "He's coming as a guest?" She winced at the note of surprise in her voice.

Jaya laid a gentle hand on Anya's arm. "Apparently so. Rohan Kapoor—you remember him, Sameer's college friend?—he booked two spots for this retreat. One for himself, one for Sameer. I guess they're coming together." Jaya bit her lip, eyes searching Anya's face with concern. "I only realized it late last night when I was reviewing the arrival schedules. I… I didn't know how to tell you."

Anya exhaled slowly, her breath noticeably unsteady for just a moment. The Western Ghats' morning chorus of cicadas and distant bird calls seemed to fade under the roar of memory in her ears. "It's been years," she said quietly, as much to herself as to Jaya. Years since she had last seen Sameer Malhotra. Years since she'd heard his voice, which used to speak her name with such affection. Her gaze drifted out over the valley, unfocused, as the past came rushing back in an unstoppable wave.

MUMBAI—FIVE YEARS AGO

Monsoon rain drummed against the glossy leaves of the gulmohar trees lining the quiet Mumbai street. A younger Anya stood under the awning of an upscale café, arms wrapped around herself as she watched the downpour. Her silk dupatta was already damp from the humidity and clinging to her thin shoulders. The moisture in her eyes threatened to spill over—whether it was rain or tears, she wasn't sure. She blinked hard.

Sameer stepped out of a black auto rickshaw, dashing through puddles toward the café. The moment Anya saw him, her resolve wavered. He looked exactly as he always did: a little disheveled, hair plastered to his forehead from the rain, eyes bright with warmth at seeing her. "Anya!" he called, smiling. He jogged to her side. "I'm sorry I'm late. Traffic is crazy." He flipped his wet hair with a boyish shake and took both her hands in his without a second thought.

The warmth of Sameer's fingers around hers nearly undid her. Anya swallowed and stepped back, gently extracting her hands under the pretense of brushing rain off her dress. "It's okay," she lied, voice trembling despite her effort to sound steady. "Shall we… go inside?"

They settled at a corner table inside the café. The world narrowed to the soft clink of china, the steamy swirl of two coffees between them, and the man across from Anya whose eager grin slowly faded as he noticed her silence. Sameer leaned forward, concern etched in his brow. "What's wrong? You said you needed to talk about something important."

Anya's chest tightened. How many nights had she rehearsed this moment? And now her carefully practiced words scattered like petals in the wind. She lowered her eyes to her coffee. "Sameer, my family…" she began, then faltered. The memory of her father's voice was loud in her head: *He has no stable career, no family background to speak of. You will not marry him, Anya. This engagement is a mistake.* Her mother's tears, her aunt's hushed warnings about duty and reputation—all pressed on her.

She cleared her throat and tried again, straightening her spine. "My family doesn't approve of us. Of our engagement." Each word felt like a stone dropping between them. "They… they think it's best if we call it off."

Sameer stared at her as if he hadn't heard correctly. A heavy silence hung between them, broken only by the patter of rain on the window. "What?" he finally whispered. "Anya, *we* are engaged. What do they have to do with—" He caught himself, frustration flaring in his dark eyes. "This is about your father, isn't it? He never believed I was good enough."

His voice cracked on the last two words, and Anya felt something inside her splinter in unison. She reached across the table instinctively, then stopped, fingers curling back before they could touch him. "Sameer, please understand," she said, hating the pleading tone in her voice. "I'm the eldest daughter. I owe them respect. They've… they've made sacrifices for me. I can't just run off and marry against their wishes." She bit her lip hard to keep it from trembling.

Sameer's hands balled into fists on the table. "We could wait," he said desperately. "We don't have to marry right away. Let me prove myself to them. I got the offer in California — you know I'll be earning well at the startup. Your father will see I can make a future for us." His words tumbled out in a rush, eyes searching hers for any sign of hope.

Anya looked into the eyes she loved so dearly and felt her resolve crumbling. For a moment she imagined it: holding on to Sameer, fighting for him, waiting for him to return in triumph from California. Perhaps her family would come around when they saw his success. But as quickly as hope arose, reality doused it. Her father's ultimatum was clear—if she disobeyed, she would be severing ties with her family. They had threatened to cut off all support, to consider her an outcast. At twenty-two, Anya had never defied her parents on anything. The very thought filled her with dread and guilt.

She blinked back tears and forced herself to break the gaze. "Some things can't be proved in time," she said softly. "They… they don't believe in your dreams like I do. And I can't go to America with you, Sameer. I can't leave my family and everything here." Each admission was agony, a betrayal of her own heart. "I'm sorry," Anya whispered, staring down at the diamond ring on her finger — the ring Sameer had given her in a moment of pure love and confidence in their future. The sight of it blurred through her tears.

With trembling fingers, she tugged the ring off. It felt like severing a part of herself, but she placed it gently on the table between them. "I have to do this," she said, voice barely audible over the lump in her throat. "We have to end our engagement."

Sameer looked as though she had struck him. His eyes flicked to the tiny glittering ring, then back to her face in disbelief. His voice came in a raspy denial. "No, Anya, you don't mean that." He reached for her hand across the table, grasping it tightly, almost desperately. She could feel his hand shaking. "You love me. And I love you. Isn't that worth fighting for? Don't *I* get a say?" His voice rose, drawing a glance from a nearby waiter, but Sameer didn't care. There was raw hurt and anger in his eyes now. "This isn't just your family's decision. It's ours."

Tears cascaded down her cheeks, a torrent of grief and self-castigation. "I'm so sorry," she said. She slipped her hand from his grip and wiped the wetness from her cheeks with the back of her hand. The look on Sameer's face was breaking her heart—betrayal, devastation, and disbelief all at once. "I do love you," she whispered, her composure shattering, "but I can't ruin my family. I can't be the reason my father…" She didn't finish, she couldn't. Her sobs choked off her voice.

Sameer's chair scraped harshly against the floor. He flung a few rupee notes on the table, his jaw clenched. "Fine," he said in a low, strangled voice. "If this is what you want." He snatched the ring into a tight fist. "I won't beg."

He stalked away from the table and into the rain before she could say another word. Through the rainwater weeping down the café window, she saw Sameer pause for a moment. For a second, she thought he might look back. But he squared his shoulders and disappeared into the monsoon haze and out of her life.

Anya stifled a cry. Her tears tasted of salt and bitterness. Even as her heart screamed that she'd made a terrible mistake, another voice—sounding suspiciously like her father's—whispered that it was for the best. In time her heart would heal and she would thank them for guiding her.

But heartache seldom listens to reason…and heartache was all she had.

PRESENT DAY—SHANTIVAN RETREAT

"Anya? Anya!" Jaya's voice cut through the haze of memory. Anya blinked, her eyes refocusing on the verdant valley spread out below the retreat. She realized her cheeks were damp, whether from the mountain breeze or the ghost of those old tears, she wasn't sure. She brushed her face and straightened her posture. Jaya was gazing at her with open concern. "I'm sorry," Anya said. She cleared her throat. "I… got lost in thought."

Jaya's expression softened. "You were remembering, weren't you?" she said gently. There was no need for Jaya to clarify what memory. Everyone in the family knew about the broken engagement even though it was never spoken about openly. Jaya slid an arm around Anya's shoulders in a comforting half-hug. "It was a long time ago, Di." She used the affectionate Hindi term for elder sister. "And you did what you felt you had to."

Anya managed a tight smile. "And look where it got me," she replied, trying to inject a lightness she didn't feel. "I built all this." She gestured around the exquisite retreat she had created—the fruition of years of hard work, investment, and yes, distraction from the pain. "A luxury wellness haven in the middle of nowhere. Not exactly what my parents had in mind for me either." Her tone was wry. In truth, her powerful family had been lukewarm to the idea of her striking out on her own, at least until the retreat's clientele began carrying the label "elite."

Jaya squeezed her shoulder. "They came around. Your father even boasts about Shantivan to his friends now, don't forget." She offered a conspiratorial smile. "Auntie told me he brags that his daughter is an entrepreneur providing 'world-class holistic experiences' to Bollywood stars."

Anya huffed a soft laugh despite herself. "Yes, well, success has a way of changing minds." Her father's pride in her work came only after it became a socially prestigious venture. But it was true: she had won a measure of independence and respect by building Shantivan. She'd thought she had moved on, that the choices made five years ago were firmly buried in the past.

Yet now, the past was literally coming back to her doorstep. "Jaya, does he… do you know if Sameer knows I run this retreat?" Anya asked, a note of vulnerability creeping into her voice. "Perhaps he didn't even realize." Part of her hoped he didn't know—that his appearance was a fluke, an impersonal coincidence of the wealthy wellness world. Otherwise, the idea that Sameer Malhotra might have deliberately chosen to come here, to her, was almost too much to parse.

Jaya tilted her head thoughtfully. "Rohan made the booking through our online portal. I doubt he or Sameer corresponded with us directly. But your name and photo are on the website's 'About' page, aren't they?" She gave Anya an apologetic look. "If he looked up Shantivan at all, he knows."

Anya released a breath she hadn't realized she was holding. Her heart fluttered at the thought that Sameer might have seen her photo on the site and decided to come anyway. Why? To flaunt how far he'd risen? To prove something to her, to himself? Or simply for a holiday with a friend. Perhaps he genuinely didn't care if she was here or not? That last possibility stung more than she expected.

"I suppose I'll find out soon enough," Anya said quietly. Her teacup was empty now; she set it aside and noticed a slight tremor in her hand. "Their car from Mumbai will arrive by lunchtime. I should get ready to welcome our guests."

Jaya nodded. Concern lingered in her eyes. "I'll be here," she said. "We can ask one of the managers to handle Mr. Malhotra's check-in if—"

Anya interrupted. "No." She stood taller. Her voice regained the calm, decisive tone of the Retreat's director. "No, I won't hide. I'm a professional, and he's just another guest." She smoothed an errant crease in her kurta with more force than necessary. "We'll treat him with the same courtesy we extend to everyone. That's all."

If Jaya was unconvinced, she didn't show it. She gave Anya's hand a supportive squeeze. "Alright, boss. If you insist." A hint of a teasing smile touched her lips. "But just know, if you need an emergency extraction from any awkward conversation, I'll be your knight in shining yoga pants."

Anya chuckled and shook her head. "What would I do without you?" she asked. She took a deep breath and turned.

The sun had fully risen now, burning off the last of the morning mist and revealing the vibrant greenery of the hillsides. The day was beginning in earnest, and so would the charade of her indifference.

On the way back toward the main pavilion to prepare for the guests' arrival, Anya's heart thudded in anticipation and dread. Sameer Malhotra—the only man she had ever loved—was coming into her world again after all these years. She prayed silently for the strength to keep her composure. No one, especially Sameer, could ever know how much of her calm, successful exterior was built atop the shaky foundation of what they had left behind.

CHAPTER TWO

By early afternoon, Shantivan Retreat hummed with the discreet energy of arrival day. Uniformed attendants stood ready to welcome each guest with trays of chilled tender coconut water and jasmine garlands. The gravel driveway, lined with blooming hibiscus and brass lamps, curved up to the grand entrance where Anya and Jaya waited. The main pavilion's open-air lobby was an elegant expanse of teak wood, silk cushions, and panoramic views of the valley below. A soft instrumental *sitar* melody played in the background, infusing the air with calm.

Anya greeted the first wave of guests with her trademark poise. A famed Bollywood actress stepped out of her car. Anya welcomed her with a warm smile and pressed a fragrant garland into the star's hands. Next arrived a Mumbai business tycoon and his wife, both looking grateful to escape the city's chaos. Anya smoothly checked them in, making genteel small talk about their journey and the weather. To each newcomer, she was the picture of gracious hospitality—attentive, unflappable, composed.

But with each passing minute, her eyes flickered toward the drive, searching for *him*. Anticipation set her nerves tingling under her skin. She had tied herself into a strict knot of professionalism while internally repeating *Sameer Malhotra is just another guest*. Still, her heart refused to heed logic, thudding faster every time an approaching engine sounded in the distance.

At last, a gleaming black SUV appeared between the ornate gate posts, winding up the hill toward the pavilion. Anya's breath caught. She stood a little taller, smoothing her hair and tugging once at the hem of her fitted kurta top. Beside her, Jaya followed her gaze and gave the slightest nod of solidarity. This had to be them.

The SUV rolled to a gentle stop. For a moment, all Anya could see was the reflection of palm fronds and sky on the tinted window. Then the driver opened the back door, and Sameer Malhotra stepped out onto the stone driveway.

Anya's composed mask almost slipped at the sight of him. Sameer was… changed, yet heartbreakingly familiar all at once. He was taller than she remembered—or perhaps just carried himself with a new confidence that made him seem so. Dressed in a tailored casual style, he wore dark jeans and a crisp dove-gray linen shirt rolled to the elbows, revealing strong forearms. His once boyish face had matured; a neatly trimmed beard accentuated the cut of his jaw. He pushed his sunglasses up onto his head, squinting slightly in the glare sun, and as he did, Anya saw his eyes clearly for the first time in years. Those eyes, a deep espresso brown she had once gazed into with utter love, now swept over the retreat's entrance, then toward her.

Their gazes met. A lightning bolt of memory and emotion shot through her—she wasn't ready for it. Still, ever professional, she forced a polite smile and stepped forward with practiced, near robotic elegance as Sameer and another man emerged from the car.

"Welcome to Shantivan," Anya said, thanking heaven that her voice did not quake. "I'm Anya Kapoor, the founder. It's a pleasure to have you with us." Her eyes remained on Sameer's face, trying to read his reaction. Did he feel anything? Shock, anger, indifference? His expression was cordial but guarded, a polite mask that rivaled her own.

Sameer inclined his head slightly. "Thank you," he replied in a calm, even tone. "It's… good to be here." Those words hung as if loaded with unspoken meaning. His gaze held hers a fraction longer than necessary, and Anya's stomach fluttered. Was that a flash of surprise she saw in his eyes, or just her imagination?

The man who had arrived with him cleared his throat lightly, breaking the moment. "Hi! I'm Rohan," he said. He stepped forward with an easy grin. "Rohan Kapoor. Not related to Anya, by the way," he added quickly with a friendly chuckle. Rohan was tall and broad-shouldered with a genial face. He looked between Anya and Sameer knowingly, as if sensing the undercurrents. "We're really looking forward to this retreat. Heard amazing things."

Jaya took the cue and stepped in smoothly. "Welcome, Rohan-ji," she said with a warm laugh, using the respectful suffix playfully. "I'm Jaya Singh, the operations manager here—and Anya's cousin. We're delighted you both could join us." She handed each of the men a fresh coconut with a straw, the customary welcome drink.

As Sameer accepted his, his fingers brushed Jaya's, and he offered a courteous smile. "It's a beautiful place you all have here," he said, eyes drifting to the panoramic view beyond the lobby. "The photos didn't do it justice." There was genuine appreciation in his voice, which made Anya's chest swell unexpectedly with pride. She had poured her soul into making Shantivan a sanctuary; hearing him acknowledge its beauty felt oddly personal.

"Thank you," she responded. "We like to think it's a special corner of the world." Anya kept her tone polite, but inside her emotions churned. Being this close to him—breathing in the subtle note of his cologne (sandalwood and citrus, new and sophisticated)—was almost overpowering. A dozen memories of simpler times assaulted her: Sameer taking her on a cheap scooter ride to Marine Drive, laughing in the rain; the way he'd brush a strand of hair behind her ear before he kissed her. She forced her mind back to the present with effort.

Anya gestured toward the check-in desk, where an attendant waited with keys and welcome packets. "Shall we?" she said. As they moved, she noticed Sameer walking with a slight limp, just barely perceptible. Concern flashed through her, instinctive and unwelcome. Had he injured himself? It wasn't her place to ask. She pressed her lips together and kept moving.

At the desk, formalities proceeded efficiently. The attendant confirmed their luxury cottage—a two-bedroom villa overlooking the valley—and explained the schedule: sunset yoga, an Ayurvedic dinner, the works. Anya listened while maintaining a beatific smile. Sameer's eyes flicked to her occasionally, as though he too was struggling not to stare. Each time, Anya felt her face threaten to warm, and she quelled it by concentrating on the papers.

"If there's anything you need during your stay, please don't hesitate to ask," Anya said once the check-in was complete. "We want you to feel completely relaxed and at home."

Sameer's lips curved in a polite facsimile of a smile. "You've thought of everything, I'm sure," he replied. Was that a hint of admiration in his tone? Or was she reading into things? "It's impressive... what you've built here." He added the last quietly, almost an aside, but Anya heard it loud and clear. Her heart gave a treacherous squeeze.

"Thank you," she answered, meeting his eyes directly. "That means a lot." There was a beat of silence. So many unsaid things hung between them in that brief exchange. Jaya and Rohan looked on with polite smiles, but Anya could sense Jaya's subtle tension and Rohan's curiosity.

Jaya gently broke the moment. "Let's get you settled in. I'll have your bags sent to your villa. Our welcome yoga session is at 5:00 pm by the meditation deck, if you both are up for it." She winked conspiratorially. "No pressure, though—you might just want to explore or rest. You've had a long trip."

Rohan laughed, running a hand through his hair. "Oh, we'll definitely need some yoga after sitting in that car for hours. My spine is killing me." He elbowed Sameer. "Right, Sam? Maybe some downward dog to stretch out?"

Sameer gave a half-smile. "Speak for yourself. But yes, some stretching could be good." He looked back to Anya. "We'll see you later, then." The gentle formality of his words couldn't hide the undercurrent in them. It was neither dismissal nor warmth—just careful neutrality. Anya realized that Sameer, like herself, was holding back a tide of feelings and memories under a teetering veneer of courtesy.

"Yes. Please make yourselves at home," Anya said. "I'll be around if you need anything."

She stepped back, allowing Jaya to lead Sameer and Rohan toward their villa. As the two men walked away, flanked by a porter carrying their luggage, Anya let her smile drop and exhaled.

Sameer did not glance back, but Rohan snuck a friendly wave in Anya's direction. She lifted a hand in return, grateful for the small gesture of normalcy. And then they were gone around the bend of the flower-lined path.

Anya stood in the now-quiet pavilion, her heart pounding. She had survived the initial meeting. It was polite, civil… and utterly agonizing beneath the surface. A part of her wanted to run—to retreat to her office and compose herself. But another part, one she barely dared acknowledge, was drawn to every detail of Sameer's presence. He was here, real and solid, not just a bittersweet memory. And he'd said it was good to be here, had he not?

She pressed cool fingers to her burning cheeks. This week might test her more than any meditation or yoga regimen ever could.

Jaya returned a moment later, her expression carefully non-committal until she was sure no guests lingered within earshot. Then her eyes widened and she released a whoosh of breath. "Well *that* was something," she said in a low voice. "How are you holding up?"

Anya lied automatically. "Fine," she said. Jaya raised a skeptical brow. "Okay, I will be fine. That was… easier than I expected."

She had not collapsed into a puddle, or burst into tears or a rage. They had interacted as polite strangers.

Jaya handed Anya another cup of chai proffered by a staff member. "Here. Liquid courage." She watched Anya sip, then said, "He couldn't take his eyes off you, you know. He was trying to hide it, but I saw."

Anya's hand paused mid-sip. The tea's steam wreathed her face as she glanced sharply at her cousin. "Don't be ridiculous. He was perfectly appropriate. If anything, he barely looked at me."

Jaya's lips curved. "If you say so." She linked her arm through Anya's, guiding her gently back toward the staff area. "Come. Let's go over the dinner arrangements. Focusing on work will keep your mind from spinning."

Anya let herself be led away. She couldn't resist one fleeting glance over her shoulder in the direction Sameer had gone. He was out of sight, but her heart could still sense him near, like a long-dormant compass trembling back to life and straining to find true north.

Whatever storm of emotions brewed within her, Anya resolved she would weather it. She had to—her world was watching, and so was Sameer. Five years ago, she made the most painful choice of her life. Now fate, or karma, had brought him into her orbit once more. Only time would tell if this was a second chance at the love she left behind, or another test of the strength she'd built in its absence.

CHAPTER THREE

Later that afternoon in the privacy of Jasmine Villa—one of Shantivan's most luxurious guest cottages—Sameer Malhotra gazed out of the window at the breathtaking panorama of green mountains and valleys. The tranquil scene stood in stark contrast to his reflection in the glass. Eyes burning eyes and rigid jawline betrayed the whirl of emotions within.

Behind him, Rohan flopped onto one of the plush sofas with a dramatic groan. "Mate, this place is unreal," Rohan kicked off his shoes. "I feel relaxed already. Or maybe that's the coconut water talking." He laughed, then tilted his head to study his friend. "So… that was *her*, wasn't it? *The* Anya."

Sameer's shoulders stiffened slightly at the name. He didn't turn from the window. "Yes," he said quietly. "That was Anya." The name tasted familiar, yet slightly rancid on his tongue after so long. Outside, clouds cast gentle shadows on the verdant slopes, the scenery peaceful and indifferent to the turmoil in his chest.

Rohan let out a low whistle. "Wow. I mean, I knew she founded a retreat or something, but this…" He waved around the opulent cottage—marble floors, handwoven rugs, a private plunge pool on the deck outside. "This is some next-level success. She's really made it, huh?"

Sameer turned to face Rohan and leaned back against the window frame. "She has," he said unable to keep a note of admiration out of his voice. "Shantivan is evidently a big deal." He recalled the articles he'd read about the retreat—how it attracted India's elite seeking wellness and serenity. None of them had mentioned Anya by name (the pieces he saw focused more on the celebrity clientele and the concept), so when Rohan suggested this place for a much-needed break, Sameer hadn't made any connection until he perused the website and saw *the smile* dazzling him from *The Founder's Message.* By then, backing out felt cowardly. In truth, he'd never seriously considered the possibility.

Rohan studied him. "You okay? Those were some hellacious poker faces back there from both of you." He sat up and propped his elbows on his knees. "I half-expected sparks to start flying—wasn't sure if they'd be romantic or murdery."

The corners of Sameer's mouth twitched, but he suppressed the smile. "Was it that obvious?" he asked.

He walked over and sank into an armchair across from Rohan. Running a hand through his hair, Sameer exhaled slowly. "I wasn't sure how it would feel to see her." He shook his head. "Turns out I… I'm still not sure. She was so composed, so damnably polite… like I'm a stranger."

"Well, technically, you kind of are now," Rohan said. "Five years is a long time. People change." He paused. "You've changed too, you know. You're not exactly the same heartbroken guy who hopped on that flight to San Francisco."

Sameer gave a short, humorless laugh. "Heartbroken… that's putting it mildly."

He remembered the days after Anya ended their engagement as a blur of pain and the restless pursuit of escape. He had thrown himself into work in California, determined to drown thoughts of her in lines of code and startup hustle. "I was a mess," he said. "But I told myself I'd prove her family wrong. Prove that her faith in me –" He stopped. Her faith. She *had* believed in him once, with all her heart, until fear tore them apart…or tradition…or protocol… or whatever the hell it was.

Rohan nodded with the solemnity of a priest at Confession. "And you did prove them wrong. Look at you now—founder of a unicorn startup, *Forbes* list, investors eating out of your hand." He grinned. "Hell, man, you're the poster boy for success. If this were a

Bollywood movie, you'd ride up on a white horse and show the girl what she's been missing."

Sameer's laugh was genuine this time, picturing the absurdity. "Unfortunately, life isn't a Bollywood movie," he said. "There are no convenient villains or easy resolutions." He leaned forward. "Seeing her today… it hit me that maybe she never needed rescuing. She built her own success. She looked—" He hesitated, searching for the right word. *Beautiful?* Yes, achingly so, but it was more. "She looked self-assured. Like she's doing just fine without me."

Rohan's expression softened. "Did you expect her not to be? You always said she was strong."

Sameer shrugged, a troubled crease on his brow. "I don't know what I expected. Maybe I hoped… you know…she'd be miserable. Or afraid she'd moved on with someone else." He swallowed. The thought of Anya with another man had haunted him for years, though he tried to banish it. "She's not wearing a ring." The observation slipped out before he could stop it.

Rohan raised an eyebrow. "You noticed that, huh?" When Sameer shot him a look, Rohan held up his hands. "Alright, yes, I checked too. Purely out of curiosity, mind you—the famous lost love of my buddy and all." He gave a half-smile. "No ring. So presumably not married. But that doesn't necessarily mean she's available, you know."

Sameer's jaw tightened. He stared at a pattern on the rug and tried to discern if it was a butterfly or something abstract. "No, it doesn't," he said.

For a moment, only the sounds of the rustling palms outside and bird calls filled the room. Rohan finally slapped his knees and stood up. "Well! We didn't come here to mope in a villa, did we? We came to relax and get your workaholic self some peace." He stretched. "And maybe to allow fate a chance to do its thing."

Sameer arched a brow. "Fate, huh?"

"Sure," Rohan said. "Second chances, closure, karmic balance, whatever you want to call it. You two have obviously got unfinished business. Even I felt the temperature drop a few degrees when you intentionally did not shake her hand—or was it my imagination?"

Sameer remembered how he had deliberately kept his hands clasped behind his back when they first approached, not trusting himself to touch even her hand. "No, not your imagination," he said. "Seemed…ah…safer."

Rohan walked over and squeezed Sameer's shoulder. "I get it. But man, you're here now. She's here. At least talk to her while you have the chance. What's the worst that could happen? You already survived the hardest part—seeing her again."

Sameer let out a slow breath. "Talk to her," he said. The idea made the pulse in his temples throb. *What the hell would I say—why did you break my heart? Do you still think about me?* Those were questions he'd never dare voice, not like this. "I'm not sure dredging through the past is a good idea."

"Maybe, maybe not. But you'll be around each other this whole week. Can you really avoid it?" Rohan gave him a pointed look. "Sometimes clarity is the only way to get closure. Or… a new beginning."

Sameer met his friend's gaze and offered a faint, grateful smile. "When did you get so wise?"

Rohan laughed. "Happens after doing the rounds in the start-up scene—you hear enough motivational talks; some of it sticks." He headed toward the door. "I'm going to check out the grounds, maybe find that infinity pool I saw on the brochure. You coming? We have an hour till yoga."

Sameer stood and moved back to the window for one more glance. Somewhere down the slope, beyond the swaying coconut palms, Anya was overseeing another arrival or adjusting some detail to perfect her retreat. Always so dedicated, so conscientious. He realized he felt proud of her—despite everything, despite the scar still aching in his heart.

"I'll join you in a bit," he said. "Go on ahead."

After Rohan left, Sameer lingered alone in the quiet of the villa. He let the peaceful ambience wash over him—the distant trickle of water from a fountain, the rustle of the breeze through spice trees. Closing his eyes, he took a deep breath, the scent of jasmine and lemongrass filling his lungs. This trip was meant to be a restorative escape from his high-pressure life, yet it had thrown him into the most emotionally turbulent situation he'd faced in years.

He opened his eyes and caught his reflection in the glass once more. A successful entrepreneur, confident and worldly, yes. But also a man with the weeping, open wound of a broken engagement…a fissure no achievement was going to close.

He repeated the mantra he'd used for years to dull the anger. "She did what she thought was right." He'd never been able to blame her like he wanted—but forgiving wasn't the same as forgetting.

He remembered the brief moment at the check-in when they locked eyes and she thanked him for his compliment. There'd been a flicker there beneath her cool professionalism, a shadow of a glimpse of the Anya he once knew—warm, passionate, capable of deep feeling. It was gone in an instant, but he hadn't imagined it. It was not indifference he'd seen, but restraint.

Sameer ran a hand along the windowsill, feeling the smooth wood under his fingertips, grounding himself. Perhaps Rohan was right; perhaps fate had handed him a week in this idyllic place to make peace with the past. Whether that meant a chance to rekindle what was lost or simply to say a proper goodbye, he couldn't tell yet.

Another deep breath and he stepped away from the window. He'd spotted a pathway leading toward the pool and spa. It was lined with banana plants and orchids. If he followed it, eventually he'd cross paths with Anya again—at yoga, at dinner, somewhere.

There was no avoiding it—even if he wanted to.

The tropical sun dipped into late afternoon hues. He walked out of the villa with a weighty mixture of hope and fear settling in his chest. The stage was set; they were under the same sky once more, surrounded by the healing tranquility of the Western Ghats.

He squared his shoulders much as he had five years ago when he slogged away through the rain. Once again he was walking toward something unknown. Whatever happened next, Sameer sensed this reunion—this slow collision of their worlds—would change him, for better or worse. Deep in some crevasse of his mind or heart, he wondered if the Universe would offer them a chance to discover if they were still, after everything, the marrying kind.

ACT II—SWEAT IT OUT

CHAPTER FOUR

The scent of eucalyptus hung in the air like memory itself—cool, clean, and just a little medicinal. Anya sat cross-legged at the edge of the meditation deck, her back straight, hands resting gently on her knees. In front of her, the valley stretched in hues of emerald and mist. The yoga instructor's voice, soft as the breeze, guided the group through a body scan. Yet all Anya could sense was the presence beside her: Sameer.

He was still and silent, a mirror of composure, but Anya could feel the alertness in his breath, the way his fingers flexed slightly when she shifted beside him. They weren't touching, but the mere proximity after years of distance made her pulse flutter…something for which she could not have prepared.

The day had been full of little landmines. She'd run into him by the juice bar in the morning when they both reached for a slice of papaya. They'd exchanged a polite nod, nothing more. At the garden walk, he'd lingered behind the group and paused to admire a rare butterfly—one she'd pointed out to guests a hundred times before. But hearing Sameer name it in his low, thoughtful voice—"That's a Common Nawab, isn't it?"—made it feel like the first time.

Now, with the meditation instructor bringing the session to a close, Anya kept her eyes shut a beat longer than necessary. When she opened them, Sameer was already rising smoothly. He turned toward her and hesitated, just for a second. Then:

"Good session," he said, voice neutral.

She nodded, rising as well. "Yes. The view helps."

They stood there for a moment more than they should have,

caught in that awkward pause where strangers end a conversation and ex-lovers imagine a hundred different ways to continue it.

CHAPTER FIVE

The rainstorm came suddenly as they always did in the hills. One minute the air was heavy with afternoon heat; the next, thunder rolled low and lazy across the valley, and the sky cracked open.

The group had just finished a guided herbal walk and was scattering when the downpour hit. Guests squealed and raced for shelter. Anya and Sameer, both holding bamboo umbrellas too small for a true deluge, ended up sprinting toward the same yoga hut.

They reached it laughing, breathless. Anya's dupatta was plastered to her back. Sameer's shirt clung to him like a second skin. She turned, trying to wring water from her hem, and caught him watching her.

"Old times," he said.

She blinked. "Sorry?"

He nodded toward the rain. "Monsoon season. Mumbai. You used to complain about how it always ruined your shoes."

That tugged a reluctant smile from her. "I still do. But now I can bill the resort for replacements."

Rain battered the thatched roof. They sat side by side on the low bench inside the hut, water dripping from their hair, breath still uneven.

Anya looked down at her lap. "I didn't expect you to come."

"I didn't expect to see you here either. Rohan suggested it."

She glanced at him. "So you didn't know I ran this place?"

He was quiet for a moment too long. "I saw the website. Your name. Your photo. I just didn't think I'd actually see you."

Anya exhaled slowly. "You seem well."

"I am."

He looked at her, and in his gaze was the unspoken: *Are you?*

But she didn't answer. The truth was complicated, layered, and soaking through old emotional seams like the monsoon outside.

CHAPTER SIX

Later that night, the retreat hosted its signature Truth Circle. In the candlelit yoga hall, guests sat in a circle on cushions, each given the space to share one truth about themselves. A release. A reckoning.

Rohan spoke first and told a funny story about his failed vegan cleanse. Jaya followed with a tender memory about her late grandmother's jasmine oil.

When it was Anya's turn, she hesitated. Then she began.

"I built this retreat because I needed to believe in healing," she said. "Not just the kind you do with turmeric lattes or breathwork. But the kind that happens when you stop pretending you're not hurt."

The room went still.

"There was a time I made a decision that cost me something—someone—important. I told myself it was the right thing. But I've come to learn that right and easy aren't the same."

She thought briefly of her old friend Vikram and his whirlwind engagement. How effortless he and his American girlfriend Harlow made it seem. But life hadn't given her similar clarity when it mattered most.

"Sometimes the regret doesn't fade. It just… lightens until it becomes something you can carry without drowning."

A long breath. Then silence.

CHAPTER SEVEN

Scandal arrived the next morning.

A celebrity guest's assistant was caught taking photos of another guest in the steam room. Phones were strictly prohibited in that area, and the violation threatened Shantivan's reputation for privacy.

Anya's team scrambled. The guest threatened to leave. The paparazzi were already circling.

In the midst of it, Sameer stepped in.

He spoke to the celebrity's manager, diffused the assistant's defensiveness, and drafted a discreet NDA for both parties.

"You didn't have to do that," Anya said afterward, watching the storm settle.

He shrugged. "I saw a fire. I put it out. Old habits."

She looked at him, something soft in her eyes. "Thank you. Really."

"You're welcome."

He started to walk away, then paused. "Anya. That truth you shared last night... it landed. Just so you know."

Then he was gone.

And she was left with her heartbeat echoing in the space where his presence had been.

ACT III—STILL THE ONE

CHAPTER EIGHT

The final night of the retreat brought a rare kind of hush. The guests had just finished their farewell dinner under a canopy of fairy lights strung amongst ancient banyan trees. Now, the group wandered down to the fire pit —a final ritual of letting go.

Anya stood apart from the others, watching the flicker of flames dance across the faces of her guests. She felt a rare quietness in her chest, a lull in the usual thrum of responsibility. She had survived this week—held herself steady in the presence of Sameer, handled the PR fallout, even opened up during the Truth Circle.

But what lingered was the way Sameer had looked at her after she spoke. Like he saw her—not just the polished retreat founder, but the woman she still was underneath.

He was seated near the edge of the firelight now, talking with Rohan, though his eyes kept drifting her way. Jaya gave Anya a nudge.

"Go," she whispered. "Before the fire dies and the moment passes. Besides, seasonal wedding madness is coming to Mumbai soon—you won't have time for romantic revelations then."

Anya hesitated. Then she walked.

CHAPTER NINE

"Mind if I join you?"

Sameer looked up as she approached. "Of course not."

She sat beside him on the low bench carved from a tree trunk, the fire crackling softly before them.

"I wanted to thank you again," she said. "For how you handled the whole… steam room fiasco. It could've been a disaster."

"I told you," he replied, "old habits."

They both smiled faintly, the firelight softening the distance that had lingered between them all week.

"I wasn't sure you'd speak to me again," she said.

Sameer glanced at her, the glint in his eyes somewhere between mischief and melancholy. "I wasn't sure either."

Silence stretched again, but it wasn't uncomfortable.

Anya took a breath. "I thought I was doing the right thing. Choosing family over you. Over us."

"I know," he said. "And I thought I was proving something by walking away."

She looked at him, really looked. "But did we prove anything? Or just lose years we didn't have to?"

Sameer met her gaze. "I've asked myself that more times than I care to admit."

Their hands rested inches apart on the bench. Anya shifted, brushing her fingers against his.

"I never stopped wondering… if we'd find our way back."

His fingers closed gently around hers. "I never stopped hoping."

CHAPTER TEN

They stood at the overlook the next morning. No one else. The retreat had quieted as guests packed up, cars lined the drive, and the scent of sandalwood incense floated through the air.

Sameer had his bag slung over one shoulder. "So this is goodbye again?"

Anya shook her head. "Not if we don't want it to be."

He raised an eyebrow. "Are you saying you'd visit California?"

"I'm saying," she replied, stepping closer, "that I'm not the same girl who let go without a fight."

Sameer smiled slowly, his eyes soft. "And I'm not the guy who lets pride decide everything."

She reached up, brushing a curl from his forehead. "Then maybe we're finally the right people… at the right time."

He leaned down, their foreheads resting together.

"Still the one?" he asked.

She nodded.

"Still the one."

BOMBAY
BEATRICE

A reimagining of Shakespeare's *Much Ado About Nothing*

Set in modern-day Mumbai's art scene, Bombay Beatrice retells the witty love-hate between Beatrice (Bea D'Souza, a mixed-race art curator with a viral Substack) and Benedict (Dev Mehtra), a British-born Indian street artist turned gallery darling. They find themselves caught in a web of matchmaking, ego and cultural pride.

ACT I: THE CRITICS' CANVAS

CHAPTER ONE

Bea in Black and White

Bea D'Souza didn't believe in soulmates—especially not ones who painted murals with spray cans and posted shirtless photos on Instagram under the hashtag #ArtIsResistance. As Mumbai's most unapologetically sharp-tongued art critic and curator, Bea preferred her men like she preferred her palettes: curated, minimal, and silent.

Dev Mehta was none of those things.

He was loud. Loud in his brushstrokes, loud in his politics, and loud in his ability to attract both gallery buzz and TikTok followers. A British-born Indian with a muralist's swagger and a rebel's vocabulary, Dev was the kind of artist who had once scrawled "Capitalism Killed the Canvas" on the façade of the Jaipur Modern Art Museum—and was then invited to headline their spring exhibition.

So when Bea's best friend, Lali Jain, invited her to arrange a destination wedding art show in Goa—and casually added, "Oh, by the way, Dev's doing the centerpiece mural"—Bea very nearly said no.

But Lali wasn't just a bride. She was family. She had once bailed Bea out of a disastrous gallery opening when a controversial installation had been misinterpreted as anti-nationalist. Lali had known Bea since their first year at art school in Baroda, where they bonded over a shared hatred of performative minimalism and a love for cheap rum.

And this wasn't just a wedding. It was the wedding of the year.

A three-day coastal blowout with mango trees strung in fairy lights, cocktail sangeets on floating docks, and a guest list more selective than works at an art biennale.

So Bea packed her signature black linen jumpsuits, her laptop, and the emotional armor she wore like couture. The plane ride to Goa felt like a prelude to war—or worse, a sequel.

The villa compound in Assagao was a colonial fever dream—arched doorways, blue shutters, old mosaic tiles kissed by the sea breeze. The bridal suite was named after Rani Padmavati. Bea's room? Princess Sita.

Fitting, she thought. *All the myths, none of the happy endings.*

CHAPTER TWO

Enter the Muralist

Dev Mehta knew Bea D'Souza would be in Goa. He also knew she'd walk in like a hurricane disguised as a minimalist: bold lips, severe eyeliner, clothes that never begged for attention but always earned it.

He just didn't care.

Except... he did. A little.

It had been three years since they'd seen each other in person, but everyone remembered the panel discussion in Delhi. An art roundtable turned intellectual bloodsport, with a YouTube clip titled: *Bea D'Souza vs. Dev Mehta: Who Owns the Narrative?*

She had called his work "emotional exhibitionism masquerading as commentary." He had called her curation "aesthetic gatekeeping in heels."

It had a million views. More comments. And countless memes.

Dev arrived at the Goa villa with three cans of spray paint, two linen shirts, and one mission: complete the commissioned wedding mural, avoid Bea D'Souza, and maybe sneak in a few dips in the pool.

On day one, he failed at all three.

She was at the welcome brunch, in black silk and sunglasses, dissecting the centerpiece flowers like they had personally offended her. He spotted her across the lawn and immediately tripped over a bamboo lantern.

She didn't see it. Or maybe she pretended not to.

Day two wasn't much better.

They ran into each other near the gallery barn. Dev had just finished outlining the first figures on his mural—a bold, color-drenched tribute to arranged love and artistic chaos—when Bea walked in, arms folded.

"I thought you hated weddings," she said by way of greeting.

"I thought you hated anything unsponsored by a grant," he shot back.

She smirked. "Still allergic to structure, I see."

He grinned. "Still afraid of color, I see."

And so it began. Again.

CHAPTER THREE

The Setup

Lali watched it all unfold with the delighted precision of a woman who knew how to spin drama into dopamine.

She and her fiancé Neel had always suspected that Bea and Dev were two sides of the same coin—both too clever for their own good, both too proud to admit they noticed each other, both deeply committed to the art of verbal warfare.

So she and Neel decided to intervene.

Over dinner, over chai, over carefully timed comments in earshot of the eavesdroppers, they spun a web.

With help from a mutual friend—Tara, a fashion designer with a flair for theater—and Neel's astrology-obsessed cousin Reva, they crafted a plot worthy of the Bard himself.

Reva pulled Bea aside at breakfast: "You know Dev asked for your birth time? He said your Mercury must be in Scorpio. He called you 'unreasonably magnetic.'"

Meanwhile, Neel told Dev, "I overheard Bea talking about your Jaipur protest series. She said it was 'uncomfortable in the best way.'"

All lies. All delicious.

By the end of day three, Bea was eyeing Dev with suspicion laced with curiosity.

Dev, for his part, found himself sketching silhouettes that looked alarmingly like Bea—sharp jaw, high cheekbones, eyes burning like a challenge.

And then came the mehendi party. A blur of henna, laughter, and champagne. Bea wore a navy sari that made Dev forget his own name. Dev wore a cream kurta with sleeves rolled up like a villain in a BBC period drama.

They argued about whether social media was killing nuance. They disagreed about the difference between provocation and performative rage.

And yet, when the evening ended, they left the garden walking side by side. Not touching. Not quite smiling.

But something had cracked open between them. A fissure. A flicker. A beginning.

ACT II: RUMORS IN PARADISE

CHAPTER FOUR

Spark and Spite

By day four of the wedding week, the villa compound buzzed with mehendi paste and champagne. Everyone was tanned, tipsy, and dangerously overconfident in their dancing abilities.

Bea D'Souza, in a backless emerald blouse and gold jhumkas, had just finished telling a pompous gallerist that conceptual art didn't count if it needed a footnote when Dev Mehta leaned in from behind her with a smirk.

"I liked your takedown," he murmured. "Too bad you stopped before calling him a postcolonial parasite."

She didn't look at him. "I thought I'd save that line for you."

They grinned.

The flirtation was dangerous now. Sharp, knowing. Like fencing where both participants secretly wanted to get hit.

Later in the evening by the beachside bonfire, they were seated just a little too close. Dev quoted her Substack piece on art and anonymity. Bea claimed he misunderstood her thesis. He said she wrote like someone afraid of her own heart.

She said he painted like someone desperate to be loved.

Neither walked away.

And that, more than any kiss, changed the air between them.

CHAPTER FIVE

Meera's Fall

While Bea and Dev played verbal chess, another story was unraveling under the glow of fairy lights: the deconstruction of Meera Rao.

Lali's cousin Meera was soft-spoken, art-obsessed, and hopelessly in love with Neel's cousin Arjun—a finance guy with good facial structure and terrible communication skills. They were the wedding's side romance: shy glances over chai, two-person selfies, whispered "Let's tell our parents after the reception."

But on the morning after the sangeet, a video leaked.

Just a grainy clip, shot in the dark—Meera twirling in a short lehenga, laughing, dancing with a friend who wasn't Arjun. It took no time at all for a WhatsApp auntie to declare it "inappropriate," and even less for Arjun to go cold.

Meera didn't cry. Not publicly.

But Bea saw her sitting alone at the mandap rehearsal, hennaed hands clenched in her lap, staring out at the sea like it owed her an apology.

Bea recognized the look. She had worn it once, years ago, when an anonymous source called her "an imposter with pretty hair and no edge" and the art world believed it.

She marched over to Arjun during cocktail hour.

"You believe her, right?"

Arjun flinched. "I'm just trying to figure out—"

Bea didn't let him finish. "If your instinct is to believe a rumor instead of the girl you claim to care about, then she deserves better. And so does your mother's WhatsApp group."

The next day, the video was gone. The apology was issued. The gossip died a quiet, embarrassed death.

CHAPTER SIX

Mango Lanterns and Almosts

By day six, the matchmaking scheme had spiraled beyond anyone's control.

Lali's friends were convinced Bea and Dev were in love. Bea's editor texted, asking if she was secretly dating her nemesis. Dev's sister sent him a meme that said, *When hate turns into hanging out barefoot under mango trees.*

Which, incidentally, is exactly what happened.

That evening, Bea wandered into the gallery barn to check on the mural. Dev was there, sitting cross-legged on the floor, sketching the final lines with charcoal.

She paused in the doorway. "You're almost done."

He didn't look up. "And yet it still doesn't feel finished."

Bea walked in slowly. The mural was breathtaking—two abstract lovers tangled in a swirl of color, motion, and fire. She felt something twist in her chest.

"Is it us?" she asked before she could stop herself.

Dev looked up. "Would you run if it were?"

They stared at each other for one suspended beat of breath.

"No," she said. "But I'd argue about the color choices."

He smiled. "Deal."

And under the mango tree outside, strung with lanterns and laughter and the music of distant dhol beats, Dev kissed her.

It wasn't ironic. It wasn't a dare. It was quiet, warm, and slightly clumsy—like something real trying to find its shape.

Bea didn't pull away or open her eyes.

ACT III: THE FINAL FRAME

CHAPTER SEVEN

Misdirection and Midnight Oil

Every love story has its reckoning. This one came wrapped in marigold petals and accidental honesty.

Tara—the fashion designer with a knack for mischief—couldn't keep a secret if it was stitched into a lehenga. At the tail end of a turmeric-laced brunch, with too many mimosas and too little discretion, she let it slip.

"You know we made up that thing about Dev quoting your Substack, right?" she said to Bea with a giggle. "But like, turns out it's kinda true?"

Bea blinked once. Twice. Her fingers clenched the edge of her champagne flute like it might explain the secrets of the Universe.

The crack between curiosity and caution widened.

She found Dev near the banyan tree, painting the final line of his mural—a couple locked in an abstract embrace of ink and neon.

"So it was a setup," she said.

He didn't stop painting. "Looks like it."

"Everyone lied."

Dev paused, glanced at her over his shoulder. "Yeah. But we're still here, aren't we?"

She folded her arms. "That's not the point."

He capped his paint. "Maybe not. But the point is—we believed the lie because we wanted to."

They stood in silence. It wasn't angry. It was honest. A standoff between two people who realized the spark was real, even if the match had been struck by someone else.

She broke first. "I liked the mural. For the record."

He smiled. "I liked the critique. For the record."

CHAPTER EIGHT

Mandaps and Microphones

The wedding day arrived in a symphony of coconut water, sandalwood smoke, and couture that cost more than most apartments. The mandap was framed by woven palm arches and golden orchids flown in from Thailand.

Meera looked radiant in marigold silk. Arjun, sheepish but earnest, finally made amends. He took the mic during the reception and publicly apologized.

"I believed someone else's version of you," he said, voice cracking. "I promise never to do that again."

Meera's response? "I forgive you. But I'm still doing my solo classical fusion set before we talk about anything else."

The applause nearly blew the jasmine garlands off the mandap.

Bea and Dev stood to the side, watching it all with arms crossed and hearts slightly open.

Later in the evening, they slipped out of the reception. Dev wore a black bandhgala and dirty Chuck Taylors. Bea wore a champagne-toned sari and a sarcastic smile.

They headed to a local gallery's afterparty, still debating whether NFT art was the death of intimacy or the future of rebellion. When they held hands this time, it wasn't performative.

It was the beginning of something without footnotes.

EPILOGUE

Cameo in Bombay

Weeks later, they were in Bombay. The Bollywood Oscars after-party reception sparkled with chandeliers and paparazzi flashes. The air was scented with roses and tension.

Dev and Bea arrived fashionably late, wearing matte red lipstick and a knowing look. He sported a Nehru jacket featuring a single paint stain.

They argued about a controversial new artist over samosas. Harlow, their American friend from Delhi, handed a champagne glass to Bea and spotted her still-bare ring finger.

"So," Harlow teased, "who won the debate?"

Bea just laughed and tilted her head toward Dev. "We're still painting."

ABOUT THE AUTHOR

Love Hudson-Maggio is an Atlanta-based author and entrepreneur whose storytelling blends romance, culture, and self-discovery. A former screenwriting fellow at Columbia University, she brings cinematic depth to her fiction, weaving modern love stories set across India and the American South. Her acclaimed novels Karma Under Fire and Bombay Baby explore how tradition collides with the heart's desire. When she's not writing, Love leads her marketing technology firm, mentors youth, and dreams up her next story over chai and late-night playlists.